The beats to my drum, my hip-hops,
Nyree, Tyreek, Nia', Nasir, and Tiffani.
I LOVE U!
—C. S.-M.

I'm proud of you, Connie.
—F. M.

Text copyright © 2014 by Connie Schofield-Morrison
Illustrations copyright © 2014 by Frank Morrison

First published in the United States of America in June 2014
by Bloomsbury Children's Books
www.bloomsbury.com

Bloomsbury is a registered trademark of Bloomsbury Publishing Plc

For information about permission to reproduce selections from this book, write to
Permissions, Bloomsbury Children's Books, 1385 Broadway, New York, New York 10018
Bloomsbury books may be purchased for business or promotional use. For information on bulk
purchases please contact Macmillan Corporate and Premium Sales Department at
specialmarkets@macmillan.com

Library of Congress Cataloging-in-Publication Data
Schofield-Morrison, Connie.
I got the rhythm / by Connie Schofield-Morrison ; illustrated by Frank Morrison.
pages   cm
Summary: On a trip to the park with her mother, a young girl hears a rhythm coming from the world around
her and begins to move to the beat, finally beginning an impromptu dance in which other children join her.
ISBN 978-1-61963-178-6 (hardcover) • ISBN 978-1-61963-179-3 (reinforced)
ISBN 978-1-61963-209-7 (e-book) • ISBN 978-1-61963-210-3 (e-PDF)
[1. Rhythm—Fiction. 2. Dance—Fiction. 3. Parks—Fiction.] I. Morrison, Frank, illustrator. II. Title.
PZ7.S3682Iaag 2014   [E]—dc23   2013038025

Art created with oil on canvas
Typeset in Elroy
Book design by Donna Mark and Yelena Safronova

Printed in China by C&C Offset Printing Co., Ltd., Shenzhen, Guangdong
8 10 9 7 (hardcover)
2 4 6 8 10 9 7 5 3 1 (reinforced)

All papers used by Bloomsbury Publishing, Inc., are natural, recyclable products
made from wood grown in well-managed forests. The manufacturing processes
conform to the environmental regulations of the country of origin.

I thought of a rhythm in my mind.

I heard the rhythm with my ears.

I smelled the rhythm with my nose.

I sang the rhythm with my mouth.

OOH LA LA

I caught the rhythm with my hands.

CLAP

I kept the rhythm with my fingers.

I shook a rhythm with my hips.

I walked the rhythm with my feet.

I danced to the rhythm of a drum.

BEAT

I clapped and snapped,
I tipped and tapped.
I popped and locked,
I hipped and hopped.